Thomas
Gets Tricked
and Other Stories

Based on *The Railway Series* by the Rev. W. Awdry

Photographs by Kenny McArthur, David Mitton, and
Terry Permane for Britt Allcroft's production of
Thomas the Tank Engine and Friends

A Random House PICTUREBACK®

Random House 🏠 New York

Thomas the Tank Engine & Friends A BRITT ALLCROFT COMPANY PRODUCTION Based on *The Railway Series* by the Rev W Awdry. Copyright
© Gullane (Thomas) LLC 1989. Photographs © Gullane (Thomas) Limited 1985, 1986. All rights reserved under International and Pan-American Copyright
Conventions. Published in the United States by Random House, Inc., New York, and simultaneously in Canada by Random House of Canada Limited, Toronto.
www.randomhouse.com/kids   www.thomasthetankengine.com
Library of Congress Cataloging-in-Publication Data: Thomas gets tricked and other stories / photographs by Kenny McArthur, David Mitton, and
Terry Permane for Britt Allcroft's production of Thomas the tank engine and friends. p. cm.—(A Random House pictureback) "Based on the Railway series by
the Rev. W. Awdry." SUMMARY: Thomas the Tank Engine learns not to tease the big engines and pulls his first passenger train. ISBN: 0-679-80100-6 (pbk);
0-679-90100-0 (lib. bdg.) [1. Railroads—Trains—Fiction] I. McArthur, Kenny, ill. II. Mitton, David, ill. III. Permane, Terry, ill.
IV. Awdry, W. Railway series. V. Thomas the tank engine and friends. PZ7.T36948 1989 [E]—dc20 89-8502
Manufactured in the United States of America   45 44 43 42 41 40
PICTUREBACK, RANDOM HOUSE and colophon, and PLEASE READ TO ME and colophon are registered trademarks of Random House, Inc.

Thomas Gets Tricked

Thomas is a tank engine who lives at a big station on the Island of Sodor.

He's a cheeky little engine with six small wheels, a short stumpy funnel, a short stumpy boiler, and a short stumpy dome.

He's a fussy little engine too, always pulling coaches about, ready for the big engines to take on long journeys. And when trains come in, he pulls the empty coaches away so that the big engines can go and rest.

Thomas thinks no engine works as hard as he does. He loves playing tricks on them, including Gordon, the biggest and proudest engine of all. Thomas likes to tease Gordon with his whistle.

"Wake up, lazybones. Why don't you work hard like me?"

One day after pulling the big express, Gordon had arrived back at the sidings very tired. He was just going to sleep when Thomas came up in his teasing way.

"Wake up, lazybones. Do some hard work for a change. You can't catch me!" And off Thomas ran, laughing.

Instead of going to sleep again, Gordon thought how he could get back at Thomas.

One morning Thomas wouldn't wake up. His driver
and fireman couldn't make him start. His fire went out
and there was not enough steam. It was nearly time
for the express. People were waiting, but the coaches
weren't ready.

At last Thomas started. "Oh dear! Oh dear!" he yawned.
He fussed into the station, where Gordon was waiting.

"Hurry up, you," said Gordon.

"Hurry yourself," replied Thomas.

Gordon, the proud engine, began making his plan
to teach Thomas a lesson for teasing him. Almost
before the coaches had stopped moving, Gordon
reversed quickly and was coupled to the train.

"Get in quickly, please," he whistled.

Thomas usually pushed behind the big trains to
help them start. But he was always uncoupled first.

This time Gordon started so quickly they forgot to
uncouple Thomas. Gordon's chance had come!

"Come on, come on," puffed Gordon to the coaches.

The train went faster and faster—too fast for Thomas. He wanted to stop, but he couldn't! "Peep! Peep! Stop! Stop!"

"Hurry, hurry, hurry," laughed Gordon.

"You can't get away. You can't get away," laughed the coaches.

Poor Thomas was going faster than he had ever gone before. He was out of breath and his wheels hurt him, but he had to go on.

"I shall never be the same again," he thought sadly. "My wheels will be quite worn out."

At last they stopped at a station. Thomas was uncoupled, and he felt very silly and exhausted.

Next he went onto a turntable, thinking of everyone laughing at him, and then he ran onto a siding out of the way.

"Well, little Thomas," chuckled Gordon. "Now you know what hard work means, don't you?"

Poor Thomas couldn't answer. He had no breath. He just puffed slowly away to rest and had a long, long drink.

"Maybe I don't have to tease Gordon to feel important," Thomas thought to himself. And he puffed slowly home.

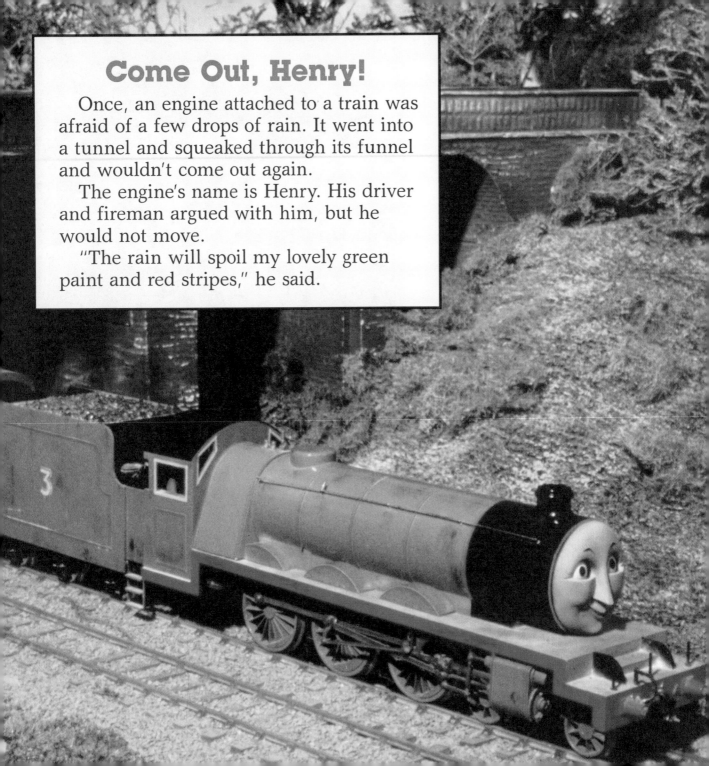

Come Out, Henry!

Once, an engine attached to a train was afraid of a few drops of rain. It went into a tunnel and squeaked through its funnel and wouldn't come out again.

The engine's name is Henry. His driver and fireman argued with him, but he would not move.

"The rain will spoil my lovely green paint and red stripes," he said.

The conductor blew his whistle till he had no more breath and waved his flag till his arms ached. But Henry still stayed in the tunnel and blew steam at him.

"I'm not going to spoil my lovely green paint and red stripes for you."

Then—along came Sir Topham Hatt, the man in charge of all the engines on the Island of Sodor.

"We will pull you out," said Sir Topham Hatt. But Henry only blew steam at him.

Everyone pulled except Sir Topham Hatt. "Because," he said, "my doctor has forbidden me to pull." But still Henry stayed in the tunnel.

Then they tried pushing from the other end. Sir Topham Hatt said, "One, two, three, push!" But he didn't help. "My doctor has forbidden me to push," he said.

They pushed and pushed and pushed. But still Henry stayed in the tunnel.

At last Thomas came along. The conductor waved
his red flag and stopped him.

Everyone argued with Henry. "Look, it has stopped
raining," they said.

"Yes, but it will begin again soon," said Henry.
"And what would become of my green paint with red
stripes then?"

Thomas pushed and puffed, and pushed as hard as
ever he could.

But still Henry stayed in the tunnel.

Eventually, even Sir Topham Hatt gave up.

"We shall take away your rails," he said, "and leave you here until you're ready to come out of the tunnel."

They took up the old rails and built a wall in front of Henry so that other engines wouldn't bump into him. All Henry could do was to watch the trains rushing through the other tunnel. He was very sad because he thought no one would ever see his lovely green paint with red stripes again.

As time went on, Edward and Gordon would often pass by.

Edward would say, "Peep, peep–hello."

And Gordon would say, "Poop, poop, poop. Serves you right."

Poor Henry had no steam to answer. His fire had gone out. Soot and dirt from the tunnel had spoiled his lovely green paint and red stripes, anyway.

How long do you think Henry will stay in the tunnel before he overcomes his fear of the rain and then decides to journey out again?

Henry to the Rescue

Gordon always pulled the big express. He was proud of being the only engine strong enough to do so. It was full of important people like Sir Topham Hatt, and Gordon was seeing how fast he could go.

"Hurry, hurry, hurry," he said.

"Trickety-trock, trickety-trock, trickety-trock," said the coaches.

In a minute Gordon
would see the tunnel where
Henry stood, bricked up
and lonely.

"Oh dear," thought Henry.
"Why did I worry about
rain spoiling my lovely coat
of paint? I'd like to come
out of the tunnel." But Henry
didn't know how to ask.

"I'm going to poop, poop at Henry," said Gordon.
He was almost there when—*Wheeeeeeeeeeshshsh*—and
there was proud Gordon going slower and slower in
a cloud of steam.

His driver stopped the train.

"What has happened to me?" asked Gordon. "I feel so weak."

"You've burst your safety valve," said the driver. "You can't pull the train anymore."

"Oh dear," said Gordon. "We were going so nicely, too. And look—there's Henry—laughing at me."

Everyone came to see Gordon.

"Humph," said Sir Topham Hatt. "These big engines are always causing me trouble. Send for another engine at once."

While the conductor went to find one, they uncoupled Gordon, who had enough puff to slink onto the siding out of the way.

Edward was the only engine left. "I'll come and try," he said.

"Pooh!" said Gordon. "That's no use. Edward can't push the train."

Kind Edward puffed and pushed and pushed and puffed, but he couldn't move the heavy coaches.

"I told you so," said Gordon. "Why not let Henry try?"

"Yes," said Sir Topham Hatt, "I will. Will you help pull this train, Henry?" he asked.

"Oh yes," said Henry.

When Henry had got up steam, he puffed out. He was dirty and covered with cobwebs. "Ooh! I'm stiff, I'm stiff," he groaned.

"Have a run to ease your joints, and find a turntable," said Sir Topham Hatt.

When Henry came back, he felt much better. Then they coupled him up.

"Peep, peep," said Edward. "I'm ready."
"Peep, peep, peep," said Henry. "So am I."
"Pull hard. We'll do it. Pull hard. We'll do it," they puffed together.

"We've done it together. We've done it together,"
said Edward and Henry.

"You've done it, hurray! You've done it, hurray!"
sang the coaches.

Everyone was excited. Sir Topham Hatt leaned out of
the window to wave at Edward and Henry, but the
train was going so fast that his hat blew off into a field
where a goat ate it for tea.

They never stopped till they came to the station at
the end of the line.

The passengers all said "Thank you," and Sir
Topham Hatt promised Henry a new coat of paint.

On their way home Edward and Henry helped
Gordon back to the shed.

All three engines are now great friends.

Henry doesn't mind the rain now. He knows that
the best way to keep his paint nice is not to run
into tunnels but to ask his driver to rub him down
when the day's work is over.

A Big Day for Thomas

Thomas the Tank Engine was grumbling to the other engines. "I spend my time pulling coaches about, ready for you to take out on journeys."

The other engines laughed.

"Why can't I pull passenger trains, too?"

"You're too impatient," they said. "You'd be sure to leave something behind."

"Rubbish," said Thomas. "I'll show you."

One night he and Henry were alone. Henry was
ill. The men worked hard, but he didn't get better.

He felt just as bad next morning.

Henry usually pulled the first train and
Thomas had to get his coaches ready.

"If Henry is ill," he thought, "perhaps I shall
pull his train."

Thomas ran to find the coaches. "Come along, come along," he fussed.

"There's plenty of time. There's plenty of time," they grumbled.

Thomas took them to the platform and wanted to run round in front at once.

But his driver wouldn't let him. "Don't be impatient, Thomas."

Thomas waited and waited.

The people got in. The conductor and stationmaster walked up and down. The porter banged the doors, and still Henry didn't come.

Thomas got more and more excited.

Sir Topham Hatt came to see what was the matter, and the conductor and the stationmaster told him about Henry.

"Find another engine," he ordered.

"There's only Thomas," they said.

"You'll have to do it then, Thomas. Be quick now!"

So Thomas ran round to the front and backed down on the coaches, ready to start.

"Let's not be impatient," said his driver. "We'll wait till everything is ready."

But Thomas was too excited to listen.

What happened then no one knows. Perhaps they forgot to couple Thomas to the train. Or perhaps the driver pulled the lever by mistake.

Anyhow, Thomas started without his coaches.

As he passed the first signal tower, men waved and shouted. But he didn't stop.

"They're waving because I'm such a splendid engine," he thought importantly. "Henry says it's hard to pull trains, but I think it's easy."

"Hurry, hurry, hurry," he puffed, pretending to be like Gordon.

"People have never seen me pulling a train before. It's nice of them to wave." And he whistled, "Peep, peep, thank you."

Then he came to a signal at "DANGER."

"Bother," he thought. "I must stop, and I was going so nicely, too. What a nuisance signals are." He blew an angry "Peep, peep" on his whistle.

The signalman ran up. "Hello, Thomas," he said. "What are you doing here?"

"I'm pulling a train," said Thomas. "Can't you see?"

"Where are your coaches, then?"

Thomas looked back. "Why, bless me," he said, "if we haven't left them behind."

"Yes," said the signalman, "you'd better go back quickly and fetch them."

Poor Thomas was so sad he nearly cried.

"Cheer up," said his driver. "Let's go back quickly and try again."

At the station all the passengers were talking at once. They were telling Sir Topham Hatt what a bad railway it was.

But when Thomas came back, they saw how sad he was and couldn't be cross.

He was coupled to the train, and this time he really pulled it.

Afterwards the other engines laughed at Thomas and said, "Look, there's Thomas, who wanted to pull a train, but forgot about the coaches." But Thomas had already learned not to make the same mistake again.